RACCOON'S PERFECT SNOWMAN

By

Katia
Wish

PUBLISHED BY SLEEPING BEAR PRESS

Raccoon was very serious about building snowmen.

All winter long he practiced.

Rolling.

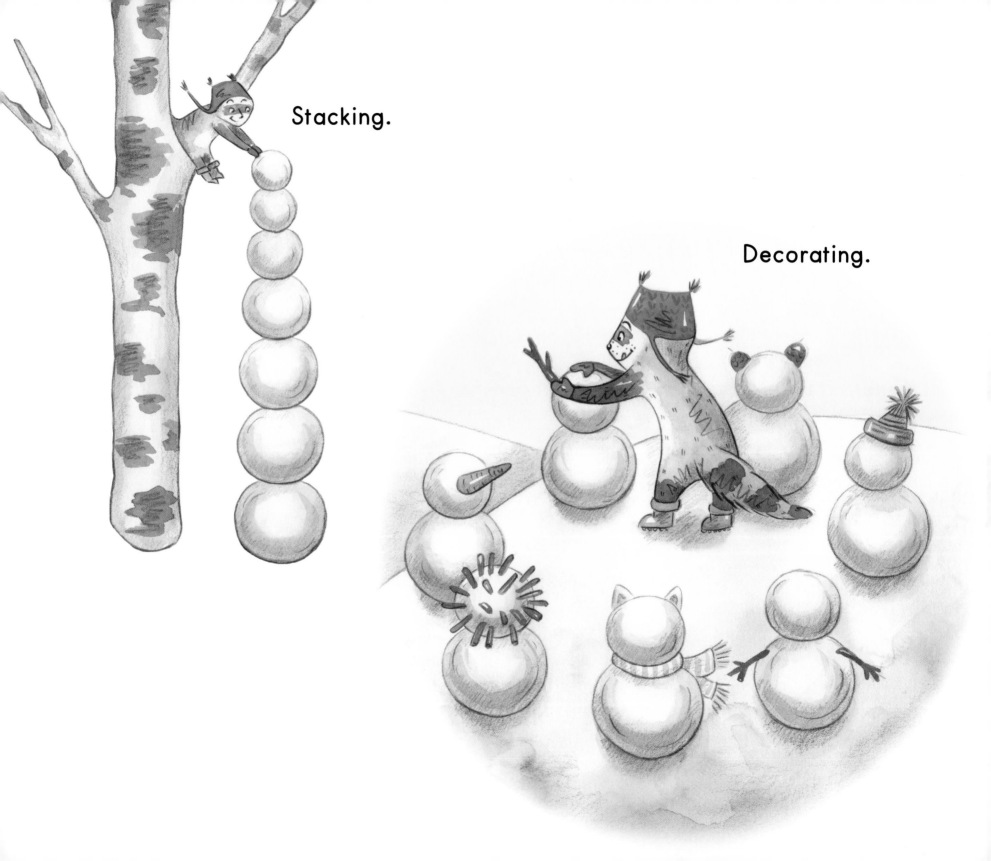

Stacking.

Decorating.

Raccoon became so good at building snowmen,
he knew his friends would want his help.

"Just do what I do. And you will have a *perfect* snowman."

Everyone got to work.

"Let's start with rolling snow," said
Raccoon. "Only use clean snow."

But Rabbit had trouble
finding the right snow.

"Next, it's time to stack! Luckily, I have all the tools we need to make perfectly even snowmen."

But Fox got tired of waiting
for Raccoon to share the tools.

"The last step is decorating your snowman."

"We have a lot of decorations."

But when Mouse looked into the sled, there wasn't much to choose from.

Raccoon admired his masterpiece.
This was the best one yet!

It was time to check on his friends' progress.

"Let's see what we have here.
Rabbit, you used dirty snow. Why?"

"Fox, your snowman is lopsided.
What happened?"

"Mouse, why is your snowman so plain?"

Then Raccoon looked back at his own snowman.

Raccoon's snowman was perfect.
But he felt *perfectly* awful.

Then he had an idea.

"Let's build one more snowman,"
Raccoon called out to his friends.

"This time, it really will be perfect!"

"Let's start rolling."

"Use any snow you can find."

"Now let's stack the snow.
Don't worry if the snowman is crooked."

"Our last step—decorations! Be creative!"

The new snowman wasn't very clean.
It didn't stand up straight.
And the decorations didn't match.

But it was *perfect*.

To Eli, my little sunshine
(Ильюше, моему солнышку)

SLEEPING BEAR PRESS™
2395 South Huron Parkway, Suite 200
Ann Arbor, MI 48104
www.sleepingbearpress.com

Printed and bound in the United States.

10 9 8 7 6 5 4 3 2 1

Library of Congress Cataloging-in-Publication Data

Names: Wish, Katia, author, illustrator.
Title: Raccoon's perfect snowman / by Katia Wish.
Description: Ann Arbor, MI : Sleeping Bear Press, [2020] | Audience: Ages 4-8.
| Summary: After perfecting the art of snowman-building, Raccoon
coaches his friends to build their own, but their imperfect creations make
everyone unhappy until they try again, working together.
Identifiers: LCCN 2020006239 | ISBN 9781534110670 (hardcover)
Subjects: CYAC: Snowmen—Fiction. | Raccoon—Fiction. | Forest animals—Fiction.
| Perfectionism (Personality trait)—Fiction. | Friendship—Fiction.
Classification: LCC PZ7.1.W593 Rac 2020 | DDC [E]—dc23
LC record available at https://lccn.loc.gov/2020006239